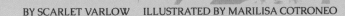
BY SCARLET VARLOW   ILLUSTRATED BY MARILISA COTRONEO

CREATURE FEATURE

BLOOD and COOKIES

Calico
An Imprint of Magic Wagon
abdobooks.com

FOR LILY AND JUDE, MY FAVORITE LITTLE MONSTERS. 'E0

WITH ALL MY LOVE TO MY FAMILY AND MY WORK. —MC

abdobooks.com

Published by Magic Wagon, a division of ABDO, PO Box 398166,
Minneapolis, Minnesota 55439. Copyright © 2020 by Abdo
Consulting Group, Inc. International copyrights reserved in all
countries. No part of this book may be reproduced in any form
without written permission from the publisher. Calico™ is
a trademark and logo of Magic Wagon.

Printed in the United States of America, North Mankato,
Minnesota.
052019
092019

Written by Scarlet Varlow
Illustrated by Marilisa Cotroneo
Edited by Bridget O'Brien
Art Directed by Candice Keimig

Library of Congress Control Number: 2018964639

Publisher's Cataloging-in-Publication Data

Names: Varlow, Scarlet, author. | Cotroneo, Marilisa, illustrator.
Title: Blood and cookies / by Scarlet Varlow; illustrated by Marilisa Cotroneo.
Description: Minneapolis, Minnesota : Magic Wagon, 2020. | Series: Creature
    feature
Summary: James discovers his grandmother has been turned into a vampire,
    and he has to protect himself and his baby sister until their mother can pick
    them up.
Identifiers: ISBN 9781532134968 (lib. bdg.) | ISBN 9781532135569 (ebook) | ISBN
    9781532135866 (Read-to-Me ebook)
Subjects: LCSH: Vampires--Juvenile fiction. | Grandmothers--Juvenile fiction. |
    Brothers and sisters--Juvenile fiction. | Babysitting--Juvenile fiction.
Classification: DDC [Fic]--dc23

TABLE OF CONTENTS

#1
GRANDMA'S HOUSE

"You're going to have a blast," Mom promised. She turned off the main road and on to the long, narrow path that eventually led to Grandma's house. "Grandma has missed you so much."

James looked out the window from where he sat in the front seat. In the back, his two-year-old sister Ruthie excitedly squealed, waving

her arms and legs in her car seat like an overturned beetle.

"Why couldn't Grandma come to our house instead?" he asked for the hundredth time since he heard that he and Ruthie would be visiting Grandma for a long weekend. "She always comes to our house!"

"Grandma's been sick lately," Mom said. "That's why we haven't seen her for a while. She's feeling better now, but she wouldn't be able to make the drive so easily. She asked if I could drop you two off."

James didn't like the idea of Grandma being sick. How much better could she be if she wasn't able to be in a car for too long?

"But we're so far away from home." He crossed his arms over his chest and gave a huff. "What if I need you?"

"It'll be fine," Mom insisted, hunching forward to peer through the windshield. "Grandma does have a phone, you know, and there's a little town just down the road. Help is nearby if you need it."

The sun had finally set, and suddenly it was very dark on the path leading to Grandma's house. There were no streetlights, or mailboxes, or any sign of life other than the beat-up dirt road they were driving on.

James couldn't imagine his sweet, happy grandma living in such a lonely and still place. Soon he could make out a house in the distance—finally, they'd made it!

"Thank goodness," James said as Mom pulled the car in front of the

house and put it into park. "One more minute on the road and I think I might have died of boredom."

"Oh please." Mom rolled her eyes and unbuckled her seat belt. "Dramatic much? You would have been just fine."

The house loomed over them. It was made with wood that had been painted yellow at one point. But a lot of the paint was faded or had chipped away over time.

James wasn't able to see into any of the windows—it was as though

they were covered by something from the inside. There was a big wooden porch that surrounded the front side of the house.

In the back seat, Ruthie growled with impatience. "Me out!" she cried. "Car off!"

James turned around in his seat, reaching over to take his sister's warm hand in his as she waved it around in distress. "Hey," he cooed. "It's okay, sis. We're gonna go inside and see Grandma now!"

Ruthie twisted her face around in

her car seat to grin, her chin shining with drool. "Gramma?"

"Yep!" Mom said, then opened the door and stepped out. "We're here!"

James got out of the car. The driveway was covered in little rocks that crunched beneath his sneakers as he walked around to the trunk. Mom handed him his backpack and suitcase, then went to unbuckle Ruthie.

"Welcome," said a voice right behind James. He couldn't help it: he screamed in surprise. He spun

around quickly, nearly falling when his shoes slid over the gravel.

"Grandma!" he cried out when he saw who was standing there. "You nearly gave me a heart attack!"

Grandma stood there, her fluffy, white hair glowing in the moonlight, laughing.

"Sorry about that, James," she said. "I was just so excited to see you pull into the driveway, I couldn't wait for you to get inside!"

"Hi, Mama," Mom said. She wrestled to close the trunk while

balancing Ruthie on one hip. "It's so good to see you! How are you feeling?"

"Much better now," Grandma said, but her smile faded a bit. "I'm so glad you're here. I'm not really

able to leave the house anymore during the day."

His heart still racing from the scare, James took in the sight of his grandmother. How did she get so close without him noticing? It was

like she'd appeared out of thin air or something.

Something even more strange was that she was wearing a long, black robe.

Grandma never wore black as far as James could remember. She'd always worn as many colors as possible, or things with flowers or animals printed on them. The last time he'd seen her in black was at his uncle's funeral.

That was his first clue that something was wrong.

#2
SOMETHING'S WRONG

"I've missed you so much, James," Grandma said, leaning down to give him a big, warm hug. As he hugged her back, he remembered all the fun he'd ever had with Grandma.

He decided that maybe the long drive had been worth it after all. She always did give the best hugs!

"I missed you too, Grandma," he said, and held her hand as they

made their way up to the house. Ruthie and Mom followed close behind. "I'm excited to see where you live."

"That's right," Grandma said, leading him up the wooden porch steps to the front door. "You haven't been here since you were a baby."

She opened the door, and James stepped inside. Immediately the smile that had bloomed when he'd hugged Grandma faded into a worried frown.

It was as dark as a cave inside

Grandma's house, almost like they were in a tomb.

The windows were covered by hastily attached wooden boards. They were draped with lovely, delicate curtains that looked dreadfully out of place framing the splintered wood.

Other than the windows, everything looked similar to what James had imagined when he'd tried to picture Grandma's house on the drive over. Everything was as neat as a pin.

There was a freshly vacuumed light blue rug and a clock that looked like a cat. A steaming tea set was in the middle of the coffee table before the TV.

19

"Why did you put those boards over your windows?" Mom asked, saying exactly what James was thinking. "I can see some of the nails sticking out!"

"Oh, that," Grandma said, nervously making her way to one of the windows. She pulled the pretty curtain over to hide the harsh sight of the wood.

"I know it sounds nutty, but it really does help keep it warmer in here at night. I just got tired of those drafts, especially when I was sick. I

20

even made new curtains to make it look less abrasive."

James wasn't sure what abrasive meant, but the boarded up windows freaked him out.

They ate dinner together, sitting around the table, Ruthie giggling as Grandma made funny faces at her. Grandma had roasted a chicken along with potatoes and green beans. James ate twice as much as he normally would.

The long drive had made him hungry for real food that wasn't the

chips and candy they'd gotten from the gas station. Grandma's cooking was exactly what he needed.

He slurped the delicious lemon garlic pan sauce from the slice of potato speared onto his fork. James noticed that Grandma hadn't taken a single bite. Worry bloomed in his stomach again as he remembered that Grandma had been sick.

After dinner, it was time for Mom to head home. She kissed Ruthie and James and pulled them into a tight hug. "You two have a great time

with Grandma," she said. "James, take care of your sister."

Her eyes darted towards the kitchen where Grandma was, and lowered her voice. "And maybe keep an eye on Grandma for me, okay?"

"I promise," James said, even though there was a nervous flutter inside that wouldn't go away.

When Mom was gone, Grandma finished cleaning the kitchen. Later, she helped Ruthie get into her pajamas and tucked her into bed alongside James in the guest room.

James liked everything about the room, except for the boarded up window. It looked like something out of a horror movie.

Everything was decorated with birds, from the bedspread to the framed paintings on the wall to the lacy curtains that adorned the wooden boards.

"Good night, little ones," Grandma sang, giving them each a kiss on the forehead. "My heart is full now that you're here. Everything is wonderful."

James eyed her black robe and nodded weakly. "We missed you too, Grandma. Are you sure you're okay?"

She smiled and took his hand. "Of course, dear," she said, but James wasn't so sure.

#3
BLOOD AND COOKIES

Grandma turned off the light, closed the door, and everything was quiet. After Ruthie fell asleep, James realized he needed to use the bathroom.

He sighed in frustration at having to leave his bed. James opened the door and tiptoed down the hall.

Through the railing at the top of the stairs, he could see Grandma

as he passed. She was sitting in the living room, watching TV and eating cookies.

James stopped when he saw what Grandma was dipping her cookies into. A tall glass of a dark red liquid that looked exactly like . . . blood!

James's eyes widened, and his jaw dropped. He remembered the way Grandma had suddenly appeared in the driveway when they'd arrived, and how she hadn't eaten anything at dinner, and how she was wearing a black robe.

27

He thought of the boards covering the windows, and how Grandma had said that she couldn't leave the house during the day. Was it possible that she'd put the boards up to block out the sunlight?

Was it possible that Grandma was a *vampire?*

He crept down some stairs for a closer look. Grandma dipped another cookie into the red liquid, giving it time to soak before raising it to her mouth. Some of the red dribbled down her chin.

28

"Curses," she mumbled, looking down to make sure none of it had gotten on her robe. "I didn't realize that blood would be so messy."

James thought he might faint from fear. It was one thing to let his imagination run wild, but she'd just said it herself. She was drinking blood!

James gasped without meaning to. Grandma turned toward where he was crouched on the stairs, his hands grasping the railing. Her face twisted in concern.

29

"James," she called. "Don't be afraid, baby. Everything's just fine."

"Grandma," he said, wondering if he was having a bad dream. "You're a vampire!"

"Come down here and I'll tell you about it." She leaned forward to set the red-filled glass on a doily

31

coaster on the coffee table. "I'm not the scary kind of vampire that you're thinking about, I promise."

"But you're drinking blood!" he said, wondering if it was possible to carry Ruthie to town. He doubted it.

"It's not from a human," Grandma promised. "It's from the butcher at the grocery store. You know me, honey, I wouldn't hurt a fly!"

James had to admit that he believed her. If she'd really wanted to drink his blood, she could have done it many times by now.

Slowly, James went downstairs and sat on the chair across from the couch. Grandma got him a plate of cookies (with a glass of milk to dip them in, not blood). Then she sat down and clasped her hands nervously on her lap.

"Remember how I was sick recently?" she said. He nodded as he ate a cookie. "Well, that was because I had been turned into a vampire. It's a shock, I know, but the exciting thing about it is that I get to live forever. With those I love."

Grandma opened her mouth and pulled her lips up with her fingers, revealing a long, pointed fang on each side of the top of her mouth.

James blinked, still hardly able to believe it. "But what about Mom? Does she know?"

"No," Grandma said, and looked at her lap. "I have to be careful about how I tell her, so that she doesn't get afraid and stay away forever. Because, you see, if I want to see my family now, they'd have to come here. Or else they'd have

to board up the windows in their own houses, which I would never ask your mother to do. I know how dreadful it looks."

She looked self-consciously to the nearest window and frowned.

James suddenly felt sad for his grandma. "Mom would never stay away from you forever, especially since you're a nice vampire."

"I was hoping that I could tell her after this visit was over," Grandma said. "If she could see it as proof that I wouldn't hurt you kids, maybe it'd

help her understand that she can still trust me."

"I won't lie." James finished his last cookie and drank the remaining milk. "I'm still freaked out. I've never heard of a nice vampire before."

"I hadn't either," Grandma admitted with a chuckle. "But then I learned that I was wrong."

"How?" James wanted to know.

"Well," Grandma said, and a little smile came over her face. "I met one. His name is Victor." Her eyes glazed over a bit. "He really is very nice."

This made him think of something else. "How'd you become a vampire in the first place, then?" he asked suspiciously.

"Victor turned me into one," she said. Suddenly, there came a lively knock on the front door. Grandma stood, her eyes bright. "Actually, that's him right now!"

#4
A VAMPIRE'S SECRET

"What?" James stood quickly, suddenly buzzing with fear. "The vampire who turned you into a vampire is *here*?"

"I told him that you and Ruthie were coming to visit," Grandma said. "But he didn't think that he'd get to meet you until tomorrow evening. It'll be such a pleasant surprise to him that you're awake. He's been

excited beyond belief to meet you, James."

James felt like he wanted to cry. He may have believed that his grandma wasn't dangerous, but he didn't know a single thing about this Victor.

Already he didn't like him on the count that he turned Grandma into a vampire. And why would Victor be excited to meet him and Ruthie?

"Do you trust me, James?" Grandma asked, coming forward and gently taking his hands in hers.

"Yes," he whispered. "I just don't think I trust Victor yet."

"If you trust *me*," she continued, "believe me when I say that Victor would never hurt you or Ruthie. I promise you that."

"Well, *I* promised Mom that I would look after you and Ruthie," he said, puffing his chest out. "Maybe you should tell Victor to go home."

"Oh, don't be silly!" Grandma said, laughing to herself as she went to the front door. "It'll be just fine, James."

40

Before he could protest, she opened the door and cried out in delight at the vision of the man in the doorway. He was older, like Grandma, and was wearing a black suit. He smiled and gave Grandma a hug before stepping inside.

"James is awake!" Grandma motioned excitedly to James. "Meet Victor."

"Hello," Victor said. He walked over to James and stuck his hand out. "It's a pleasure to meet you, young man."

41

James eyed the vampire's hand before cautiously taking it. They shook hands, and then James stuffed his hands into his pajama pockets.

Victor's eyes moved over the living room, lingering on the glass of blood that was still on the coffee table.

"James knows our secret already," Grandma said with a chuckle. "I guess I'm not so good at hiding it after all."

Victor smiled at Grandma as he went to sit on the couch. "You have nothing to hide. It's just as well that James finds out as soon as possible. Right, James?" He winked at James, who felt uneasy again.

"I guess," he said.

"I can understand how this might be a shock," Victor said. "I'm sure your grandma has let you know

that you have nothing to be afraid of. We don't kill anyone or anything, we're able to get our blood from the butcher, who would have just gotten rid of it anyway. And other than that, we want to live our lives just like you do."

"Speaking of which," Grandma said, looking at the clock. "It's getting late. We'd better get going if we want to make the most of the night."

"Going?" James crossed his arms over his stomach. "Where are you going?"

"Remember how I sneaked up on you in the driveway when you first arrived?" Grandma asked, a mischievous glint in her eyes.

"Well, that's a fun trick that I can do now that I'm a vampire. I can turn into a bat and fly!"

James imagined how fun it would be to fly through the night as a bat, going in circles and sweeps in the starry sky. "No fair!" he said.

Grandma chuckled. "If you're thinking about asking to become a vampire, the answer is no. You're

far too young. Maybe when you're old like me, we can talk about it."

James laughed, but then noticed Victor staring at him in a curious way. Unsettled, he went to the stairs.

"I guess I'll go back to bed. Thanks for the cookies, Grandma. It was nice meeting you, Victor. Erm . . . have fun being a bat, I guess."

Grandma followed him up the stairs to tuck him in again. Victor waited downstairs.

"Good night, my sweetheart," she whispered, as to not wake up Ruthie.

"I'll see you in the morning. We're going to have the best visit ever."

"Grandma," James whispered back. "Are you sure you can trust Victor? Why would he come after you to make you a vampire in the first place? It doesn't seem fair."

"I wanted to become one," she said, and took a deep breath. "But that's a story for another time, I guess. Just know that Victor takes good care of me. He always has."

But haven't you only known him for a short time? James wanted to

ask, but thought it was best to save his questions for tomorrow.

"If you say so," he said.

Grandma gave James a kiss and went to the doorway.

"Sleep well," she said. "I'll be back by the time you wake up in the morning."

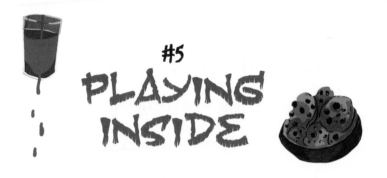

#5
PLAYING
INSIDE

In the morning, Grandma was downstairs again, just like she'd promised. Ruthie screeched happily at the blueberry pancakes waiting on the table in a big, fluffy pile.

They also had turkey bacon and orange juice. James smiled at Grandma as she watched them eat.

"Did you have fun last night?" he asked. "Being a bat?"

Ruthie giggled, her mouth full of pancake.

"Oh yes," Grandma said, and a dreamy look came over her face. "Victor and I always have the greatest time together."

"What did you do?" James was curious. "Do you just fly around all night? Doesn't that make you feel tired?"

"Well," Grandma replied. "We feed."

James felt that nervous rush inside again. "I thought you said

you only get your . . ." He looked at Ruthie, who was listening intently. ". . . your food, from the butcher at the grocery store."

Grandma gave him a reassuring smile and reached forward to pat James's hand.

"We do," she said. "But also, at night, we can turn into bats and go find a field of cows. We drink a tiny

bit from each cow and then move on. It doesn't hurt them, they can't feel it. If they're sleeping, they don't even wake up!"

She giggled at the memory. "And then, yes, we fly. The moonlight feels better than any amount of sun ever could."

James frowned at the thought. "It's sad that you'll never be able to enjoy a sunny day at the beach again. Didn't you think of that when you told Victor that you wanted to become a vampire?"

"Of course," Grandma answered, standing to clear the dirty plates now that breakfast was over. "But I can still go to the beach at night.

54

I'm happy with the decision I made, James. I hope over time, you can learn to be happy with it too."

He thought about it for a minute. If it didn't bother Grandma that she couldn't go out into the sun anymore, maybe it shouldn't bother him either. James knew he should try to understand better instead of assuming the worst things.

"Are you going to wear that black robe forever?" he asked, curious. "It does look like something a vampire would wear."

Grandma smiled at this, and swirled around so that her dress lifted out behind her.

"I think I will," she said. "Victor gave it to me on my first night as a vampire. It hides my body when I'm transforming, because it might look a little scary if it wasn't covered up. All those bones changing and rearranging into bat mode."

She chuckled. "The sound is quite startling at first."

James shivered at the thought. Still, he loved his grandma so much.

He decided to try as hard as he could to be happy about her newfound state.

All morning they played games inside the dark house with Ruthie—hide-and-seek, tic-tac-toe, and charades. After lunch, Grandma enlisted James and Ruthie's help to straighten up the house.

As a reward for doing such a good job, she announced they would make cookies afterward.

"Most food doesn't look appealing to me," Grandma said. She winked

at James as she poured oats into the mixing bowl. "But I still have to have my cookies!"

James laughed. "I could never give up cookies either."

"Yummy!" Ruthie said, straining to reach her finger around the mixing bowl to get a bit of dough. "Yummy cookies!"

"That's all you get," Grandma told Ruthie, rubbing the girl's cheek. "You'll have to wait until it's cooked to eat more!"

As the cookies finished baking,

there came the low roll of thunder, and it started raining outside.

"Perfect weather for a movie date!" Grandma said. She got a pile of pillows and blankets, arranging them in front of the TV. They watched movies until dinner. After a bath and a story, Ruthie was fast asleep in the guest room.

"Is Victor coming tonight?" James asked, uneasy. "Are you going to go out flying again?"

"Yes," Grandma said, leaning down to kiss him as she pulled the

covers up to his chin. "We spend every night together."

"Grandma," James whispered. "How did you meet a vampire?"

Grandma paused, as though she wasn't sure how to explain, and sat on the bed. "I knew him long ago, when he was a human. But I hadn't seen him since then, and I missed him so much."

She gave James a tired half-smile and ran her fingers through his hair. "I'll explain it more some day," she promised.

"But I want you to use this visit as a way to get used to the idea that I'm a vampire. Don't worry about Victor for now. You can learn more about him on the next visit."

Instead of feeling better, James felt even more concerned. Was Victor really going to stay around *forever*? It felt unfair—Grandma was his and Ruthie's and Mom's family, not Victor's!

"I'll see you in the morning," Grandma sang, and turned off the light. "Good night, my sweetheart."

#6
VICTOR'S
VISIT

The next evening, Grandma told James that Victor was coming over early, before Ruthie was asleep, so that he could meet her.

"Why does he want to meet her?" James asked, not liking the idea. "What if he tries to drink her blood?"

Across the room, Ruthie knit her eyebrows together in concentration as she colored a picture at the table.

Grandma had combed her hair into a thick braid after bath time. She looked more adorable than usual.

"Don't you dare say that," Grandma scolded James. "I have already told you that Victor would never hurt you or Ruthie!"

James felt bad for upsetting her. He could tell she really wanted him to like Victor, so he thought he'd better try harder for her sake.

Still, he'd have to make sure to keep an extra close eye on Ruthie when Victor was over.

Within ten minutes of sunset, there came the same lively knock that Victor had used the night James discovered that Grandma was a vampire. The older man stepped inside, greeting Grandma and James.

Then he slowly made his way over to where Ruthie was coloring. She looked up at Victor with big, curious eyes. "Hi!" she squeaked with a smile. "I coloring!"

"I see," Victor said, his voice deep and smooth. "You are doing

an excellent job, little Ruthie! What artistic skills you have, just like your grandma."

How would you know, James wanted to say sarcastically, but he resisted.

Ruthie was enchanted by Victor. She started following him around everywhere. When they sat down in the living room, she crawled up on the couch and sat beside him.

"Well," Victor said as Ruthie hugged his arm. "You're every bit as sweet as your grandma said."

"What'd she say about me?" James asked. He crossed his arms, realizing he was worried about Ruthie. Why was Victor so fascinated with them?

"You're smart," Victor replied. "She said that you're cautious, and rightly so, my boy. It must be scary to know vampires exist."

James felt his face get warm. Victor had him figured out.

"I guess it's scarier to imagine why someone would suddenly decide that he wants to be a part of my grandma's family after he made her into a vampire," James said. Grandma frowned at his words.

"James!" She lifted a hand to her chest. "For goodness' sake!"

"It's okay, honey," Victor said, giving her a smile. Ruthie watched James from where she sat hugging the old man's arm, her eyes wide

in confusion. "It's a perfectly understandable question."

"James mad," Ruthie said with a growl.

James lifted his chin. "Am not," he said, but he knew it was a lie.

"I'll be happy to answer your question some day," Victor assured him. "But for now, I think the best thing for you to do is understand that I have no interest in causing harm to your family.

"Your grandma and I thought maybe it'd be easier if I was around

during the day, too, to give us more time together. After we return from our nightly flight, I'll stay here, and I'll see you in the morning."

"That's not necessary," James said, starting to feel panicked. He did not want to be trapped inside with Victor all day! "I believe you."

"It apparently is very necessary." Grandma stood up. "You're only here for two more days. And it's really important to me that you understand before your mom comes that Victor is trustworthy. It's time

70

for bed now. There will be no more questions tonight."

James could tell that Grandma wasn't happy. He hung his head in shame as he followed her upstairs to the guest room.

"I'm sorry," he tried to say as Grandma tucked him in bed. She cut him off.

"Don't apologize," she said, although she was not smiling. "Tomorrow will be better. It has to be. We're running out of time, I'm afraid."

She turned off the light and shut the door. A few minutes later, James heard the frenzied squeaks of two bats as they flew past the window and into the dark, cold night.

#7
CAN WE GO HOME NOW?

Victor was downstairs with Grandma in the morning just like he said he'd be. James wished that the visit would end early and Mom would come pick him and Ruthie up right away.

He pretended to be okay with everything for Grandma's sake. But James couldn't help feel panicked whenever Victor would go out of

his way to make Ruthie laugh or whisper in Grandma's ear.

What if Victor was the bad kind of vampire, and Grandma didn't know it yet? And he was going to somehow convince her to change Ruthie into one too?

James kept a close eye on Victor all day, just in case. The old man read books to Ruthie and made Grandma laugh and laugh.

After dinner was finished, Victor offered to teach James how to play poker. But James pretended to feel sick so he could lay down on the couch.

"Are you sure you're alright?" Grandma asked, concerned as she put a cold washcloth on his forehead. "You do look pale."

"Fine," James croaked in the voice he used when he tried to convince Mom to let him stay home from school. "I just need to rest for a bit."

"Should you sleep in your bed?" Victor suggested. "So we don't keep you awake with our noise down here? It's almost bedtime anyway."

The last thing James wanted to do was leave Ruthie and Grandma alone with Victor. "I'll be fine," he said coldly, and Victor frowned.

James closed his eyes to continue on with the act, but he hadn't realized how tired he was. Before he knew it, he fell asleep for real.

He awoke to the sound of Ruthie crying. He sat up so quickly that the washcloth fell to the floor.

"Ruthie?" he cried out, looking around in panic. "What's going on?"

"It's okay, James," Grandma said

from behind the couch. "She'll be fine."

James looked toward the kitchen, where Victor was holding a crying Ruthie as he lifted her to sit on the counter. The little girl's face was red and shining with tears.

She was holding her finger in front of her, a tiny red bead of blood blooming over the tip. In the light of the kitchen, James could see the glint of Victor's fangs.

"What are you doing to her?" James yelled, running to his sister.

Grandma stopped him. "Ruthie got a paper cut on her finger," she said. James tried to pull himself out of her arms. "Victor is going to clean it and bandage it!"

James breathed hard as he watched. Sure enough, Victor was running cold water from the sink and talking Ruthie through sticking her finger into the stream.

After the finger was clean and dry, Victor slowly wrapped a bandage around it. He moved Ruthie to a chair at the kitchen table.

James decided that he'd had enough. "Don't you see?" He tugged on Grandma's arm as he pleaded with her to understand.

"Now that he's seen Ruthie's blood, and probably smelled it, he's going to want to eat her! I just know it! He might even try to get you to try it too. You can't believe him—"

"James," Grandma said. "You've got to stop. Your mother is coming to pick you up tomorrow . . ."

"Good!" James hollered. "I wish she'd come tonight!"

Then he realized: he could call Mom and ask her to come get them early. He could call her right that very minute, never mind that it was getting late.

He was sure his mom wouldn't mind making the long drive through the night if it meant saving his and Ruthie's lives. James watched as Victor eyed him suspiciously, as though reading his mind.

Without thinking about it for a moment longer, James sprang into action and ran for the telephone.

"Just wait until my mom hears about you," he said to Victor as he dialed. "There's no way she'll wait until tomorrow to come get us."

James waited for Mom to pick up. Before she could, Victor took a few calm steps forward and ripped the cord out of the bottom of the phone from where it hung on the wall.

"I'm so sorry, James," Victor said sadly. "But I can't let you do that."

"James, please," Grandma said, opening her arms for him. "Nobody is going to hurt you or your sister."

But James ran over to where Ruthie sat at the table and got her down. "Leave us alone!" he nearly yelled.

Ruthie looked confused as James pulled her toward the stairs. On the way, he grabbed a garlic clove from Grandma's root vegetable basket on the counter. Didn't vampires hate garlic?

"We're going to bed," he said. "Don't try to follow us!"

In the guest room, James tucked Ruthie in bed. He got in beside her and sat up against the headboard.

He could hear Grandma and Victor talking in low, concerned voices on the other side of the closed

door. "Should we go in?" Victor murmured. "I hate the idea of him scared and alone."

"No. Let them be," Grandma whispered in a gloomy voice. "He's had enough. I should have never done it like this."

James waited, garlic in hand, for them to come and get him and Ruthie. But nobody came.

His eyelids got heavier and heavier. Before he knew it, James had fallen asleep again.

#8
TWO APOLOGIES

When he woke up, Grandma was sitting on the end of the bed. It looked like she had been crying, her eyes red-rimmed and wet. Victor was nowhere to be seen.

"Where is he?" James whispered, as to not wake Ruthie.

"I sent him away," Grandma said. She looked to her lap, where

her hands were clasped. "It was clear that no matter what we did or said, you just weren't capable of accepting Victor. And I understand, I promise I do. It was silly of me to hope otherwise."

Grandma let out a long, tired sigh. James remembered trying to call Mom, how Victor had pulled the cord out of the phone, and how badly that had scared him.

"I just couldn't trust him, Grandma," James said. "Victor stopped me from calling Mom!

88

Why would he do that if he wasn't dangerous?"

"He absolutely shouldn't have," Grandma agreed. "He did it for me though. To protect me."

He remembered her worrying about Mom staying away, and bit his lip. He had to admit, if he'd called her late at night crying and freaking out about a vampire, Mom would probably be less than thrilled with Grandma.

It could have ruined any future chances he'd have to come back.

James wasn't sure what to say. Beside him, Ruthie snored, then turned over, sucking her thumb. He thought about the fun they'd had with Grandma until Victor had showed up.

Although, if he was being honest, Ruthie had still had fun after Victor came. It had been him who'd been resisting the trust. But the man had turned his sweet grandma into a *vampire!*

"I'm sorry I freaked last night," he said. "I guess I'm still getting used

to the whole vampire thing. Seeing you dip your cookies into a glass of blood was kind of awful—"

"I should be the one apologizing," Grandma cut him off.

"I think I made a mistake having you come at all. It wasn't fair to put you in a position where you believed your life, or Ruthie's life, might be in danger. I was being selfish. I should be ashamed of myself. And I am, James, I am."

From outside came the sound of birds chirping, muffled by the

boards nailed over the windows. It must have been morning, even if it was still dark inside.

"Your mom will be here to pick you up after lunch," Grandma said, standing and smoothing out the fabric of her long, black robe.

"Victor is gone, so you don't have to be afraid to come down and enjoy your last day here."

She gave a small, lifeless smile. "I'd love to spend as much time with you as possible. I'm going to go make some banana caramel waffles."

Even when she was sad, Grandma was still concerned about making James feel happy at her house. She'd always been like that, long before she ever became a vampire.

Maybe some things never changed. James sat in silence after Grandma left the room, thinking.

Yes, he decided at last. *I know exactly what I will do when Mom comes.*

#9
TO
TELL
OR NOT

Ruthie kept looking for Victor. She whined whenever Grandma told her that he was gone.

James made silly faces at Ruthie until she was smiling again. Then he cleaned the house for Grandma without being asked to, hoping to cheer her up.

He kept asking himself if he wanted to ever come back to the

boarded up house that sometimes felt like a tomb.

He thought that it probably wasn't normal to have a vampire for a Grandma, which meant he couldn't really ask for advice from anyone else about what to do.

When James finished cleaning, his neck was damp with sweat. Grandma thanked him by making his favorite lunch from when he was Ruthie's age—macaroni and cheese with hot dog pieces stirred in. She even drizzled ketchup on top.

Grandma watched the kids eat and took sips from the thermos in her hand. James knew it was probably filled with blood from the butcher.

"Do you ever miss eating real food?" James asked after Grandma took a drink from the thermos. "Does . . . that stuff you're drinking . . . does it taste awful?"

"It's the strangest thing," Grandma said. "But no, it doesn't. It never tastes the same way twice. It's far less horrible than I originally

96

imagined it'd be. And as for food, well, I can still eat it if I want, but the only thing I really enjoy is a good plate of cookies."

James smiled a little. "Take it as proof that you're the best cookie maker in the world. Not even vampires can resist them!"

They laughed together. James loved seeing his grandma with a real smile again, not a nervous, forced one.

Once their laughter faded away, though, she frowned a bit and

turned toward the kitchen sink. He couldn't see her face.

"I've decided to tell your mother about me tonight," she said. "I was going to do it in person the next time you came, but that might not happen now. And I don't want you to feel like you have to keep my secret, that isn't right. So after you're home, I will call her."

James tried as hard as he could to imagine what Mom's reaction would be to such news, but he couldn't. Would she laugh? Cry? Be upset?

"You're still the same you." James suddenly felt confused about everything all over again.

"I did this all wrong," Grandma said tearfully. "I'm so sorry again about how everything happened. It was unfair."

Suddenly, there came a knock on the front door. At first, James thought it was Victor. But then he remembered that it was daytime, and vampires can only go out at night.

"Mom's here!" He realized out

loud, then jumped from the table and ran happily to answer the door.

"Hello!" Mom said as she came in, giving James a big hug and kiss. "I missed my babies so much!"

"Mama!" Ruthie hopped down from her booster seat and scurried over to join the hug. "I had fun!"

"Oh, did you?" Mom said, tucking Ruthie's hair behind her ear. "Tell me all about it."

James looked at Grandma, who waited until the front door was closed to step into the living room.

She was looking at everybody in a sad way, as though she feared it would be the last time she saw them.

"You sure do have some great kids," Grandma said. She hugged Ruthie extra tight as James was getting his shoes on. "I hope you'll come back soon. There's somebody that I want you to meet."

"Who?" Mom asked, pulling Ruthie's shoes on. "Did you find a boyfriend after all these years?"

James thought of how happy Grandma was whenever Victor had

been near. How she'd smiled wide enough to show her fangs.

"Something like that." Grandma looked down sadly.

"I think you'll really like him, Mom," James said. Grandma looked to him in surprise. He winked at her. "He was very nice. Ruthie especially loved him."

"The kids met him already, huh?" Mom said with a grin. "Must be serious."

"Yes," Grandma agreed. "It really is. I think if you ever decide to meet

him, you'll be pleasantly surprised. He already knows so much about you, dear."

Mom nodded politely as she helped Ruthie get her jacket on. "Sounds good to me! I've always hated the idea of you alone out here."

James agreed with Mom. When he hugged Grandma goodbye, he whispered in her ear.

"Don't worry. I'll make sure to convince Mom that it's safe here if she ever doubts it."

Grandma's eyes welled up, and she squeezed James tight. She always did give the best hugs.

"Thank you, James," she said. "I am the luckiest Grandma in the world."

#10
A SURPRISE DISCOVERY

At home, James couldn't stop thinking about Grandma. He knew she'd be calling soon, to tell Mom that she was a vampire.

He couldn't help but feel a little nervous. Would Mom react out of fear, like he'd done? He thought maybe he should help out by reminding Mom how much she loved Grandma.

"Hey, Mom," he said as she came downstairs in her pajamas and slippers. "Can we look through old pictures of you and Grandma together?"

Mom sank into the couch, sighing as she put her feet up. "That sounds nice," she said. "Go ahead and bring one over. The albums are on the shelf next to the television."

James looked through the shelf. The ones he'd ever looked at were near the front. They were the ones that had been started when Mom

was pregnant with him. Behind those though, were the albums from before that.

He brought one over and they started to look through it. There were pictures of Mom as a baby, then a kid, then a teenager, then a college student.

James turned the page to see a photo of Mom in her dorm room. He gasped. There was a man standing next to Mom, his arm wrapped around her as they both smiled.

Victor.

"You know him?" James blurted, unable to stop himself.

Mom smiled, tracing her finger along the edge of the photograph. "I sure do," she said. "That's my dad."

James's mouth opened at the news. "Your dad?"

"Yes," Mom answered, and suddenly looked sad. "He died about fifteen years ago, before you were born."

If Victor was Mom's dad, that meant that he was James and Ruthie's *grandfather!*

"He went for a walk in the woods behind Grandma's house and never came back," she went on, frowning. "He was found a few days later, in the woods, with strange bite marks on his neck. They told us he was attacked by an animal."

In the kitchen, the phone rang. Mom stood, leaving

the photo album laying open on the coffee table.

"I bet that's Grandma now," she said, and went to answer the phone. "She mentioned on my way out that there was something important she needed to tell me."